A Camping Spree with Mr. Magee

To my wife, Lori, who makes me a very happy camper

ISBN 0-439-85576-4

Published by Scholastic Inc., 557 Broadway, New York, NY 10012, by arrangement with Chronicle Books. SCHOLASTIC and associated logos are trademarks and/or registered trademarks of Scholastic Inc.

12 11 10 9 8 7 6 5 4 3 2 6 7 8 9 10/0

Printed in the U.S.A. 40

First Scholastic printing, May 2006

Book design by Kristine Brogno and Jessica Dacher

Typeset in Filosofia

The illustrations in this book were rendered in gouache.

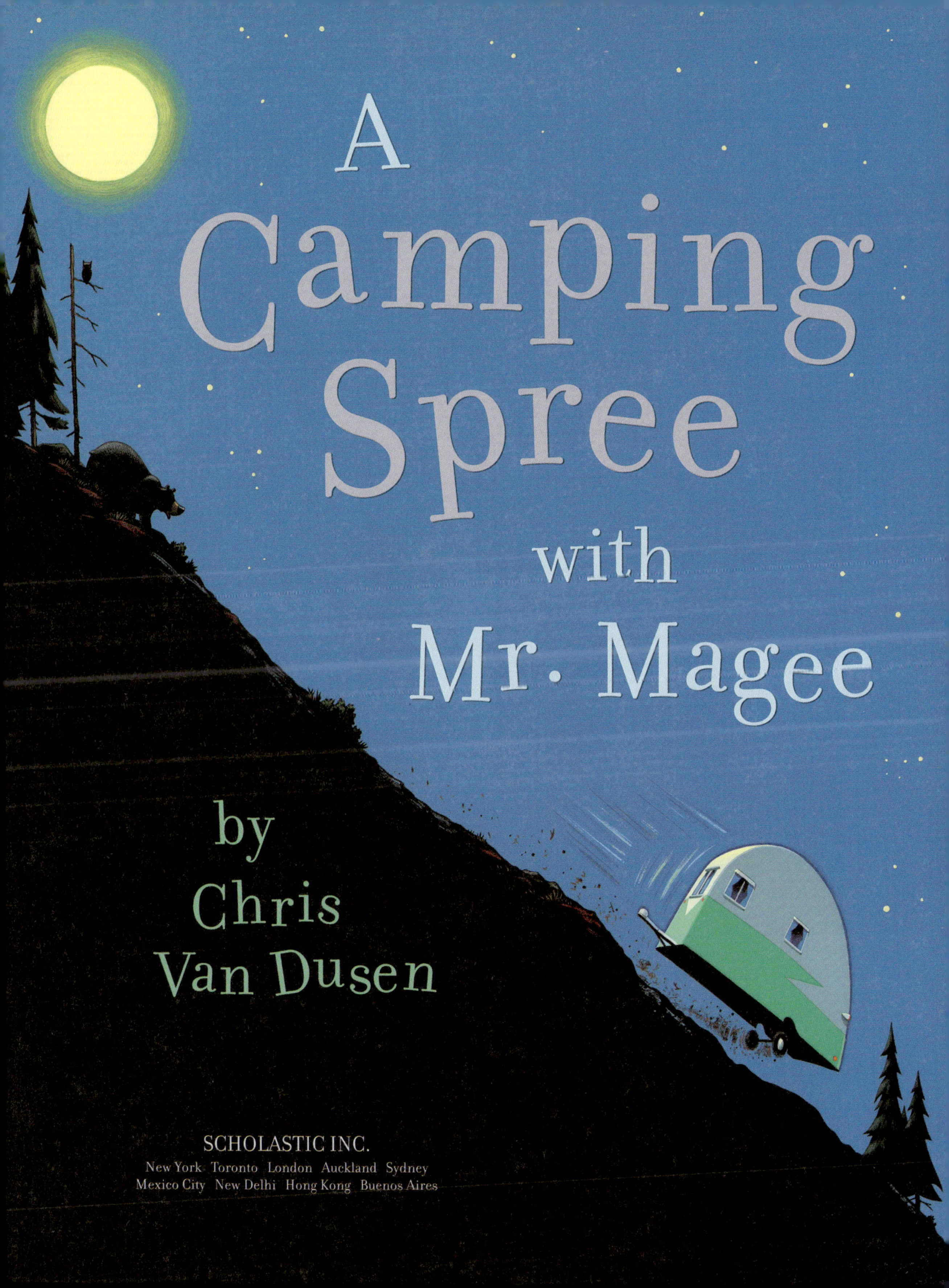

A Camping Spree with Mr. Magee

by

Chris Van Dusen

SCHOLASTIC INC.
New York Toronto London Auckland Sydney
Mexico City New Delhi Hong Kong Buenos Aires

Early one morning at 7:03,

MR. MAGEE and his little dog, DEE,

Packed up the camper and hitched up the load,

Hopped in the Rambler and then hit the road.

They drove to the mountains, far from the sea,

For two nights of camping (or possibly three).

"There's nothing like camping," said Mr. Magee.
"I know you will love it. Just you wait and see.
The views are fantastic! There's hardly a sound.
Aside from the wildlife, there's no one around.
And the air is so sweet, you'll sleep like a log,"
Said Mr. Magee to his small spotted dog.

A few hours later, they took a sharp right
And found a great spot to lay camp for the night.
It was high on a hill, with a beautiful view
Of Mt. Adams, Mt. Lincoln and Jefferson, too!
But perhaps the most wonderful feature of all
Was the brook that ran over a steep waterfall.

DEE gathered pinecones and branches and logs.
MAGEE made a campfire and cooked some hot dogs.
And as the sun set behind far distant knolls,
They sat roasting marshmallows over the coals.

As the embers went out, they felt tired and dozy,
So they climbed in their bunk beds, all comfy and cozy.
But while they were falling asleep without care,
Along came a stumbling, bumbling bear.
A kindly old bear whose sight wasn't so clear.
(He couldn't see far and he couldn't see near.)
But he could smell marshmallows, sticky and sweet.
This smell made him hungry. He wanted a treat!

He sniffed out the place where the marshmallows lay,
But the car and the camper were in the bear's way.
Yet that didn't stop the sneaky old snitch—
He simply tried squeezing right under the hitch.
And as he was shimmying into the gap,
He pushed up the hitch, which let go with a snap!

Now that the camper and car were untied,
They started to roll down the rocky hillside.
The car bounced away on the old logging road,
While the camper was heading to where the stream flowed.
It flew down the hill in a wild, bumpy ride,
With Dee and Magee sleeping soundly inside.

They were snoring and snoozing, enjoying a dream,
When SPLASH went the camper right into the stream!

The splash shook the camper. They bumped out of bed.
"Now what in the world was *that*?" MAGEE said.
And when he looked out and saw where they were,
His hair stood on end and so did DEE'S fur!
They were caught in the rapids—but that wasn't all.
They were headed smack dab for the big waterfall!

DEE and MAGEE both started to quiver,
As faster and faster they headed downriver.
But just when they thought they'd fall over the edge . . .

Their camper got stuck on a rock at the ledge.

So there they were, stranded, MAGEE and his pup,
On the top of a waterfall, fifty feet up!

Meanwhile that nearsighted bear from before
Was searching for one little marshmallow more.
When lo and behold, as if out of a dream,
He spied something sweet floating over the stream.
(But what the bear thought was a marshmallow treat
Was really the hitch and not something to eat.)

The bear was determined to capture his prize,
So he jumped in the water right up to his thighs.
He splashed through the stream to the edge of the fall
And snatched up the trailer hitch, camper and all.

DEE felt a tug! MAGEE heard a knock,
As the bear pulled the camper right off of the rock.
He dragged them both all the way back to the bank,
When he realized the hitch was *not* sweet, but quite rank!
He spit out the hitch and left in dismay—
While MAGEE and DEE'S camper again rolled away!
It flew down the path
with a jolt and a jar . . .

And stopped in some bushes—right next to the car.
Dee popped her head out. Magee looked out, too.
Had they really stopped rolling? Could it be true?
At last things were quiet and peaceful and still.
They hooked up the hitch and drove off down the hill.

And on the way home Magee said to Dee,
"That trip wasn't quite like I thought it would be."
So when they got home, with the sky turning red,

They decided to camp in the backyard instead.